Loretta and the Little Fairy

Loretta and the Little Fairy

by Gerda Marie Scheidl

PICTURES BY

Christa Unzner-Fischer

TRANSLATED BY
J. Alison James

North-South Books

NEW YORK

First published in the United States, Great Britain, Canada,
Australia, and New Zealand in 1993 by North-South Books,
an imprint of Nord-Süd Verlag AG, Gossau Zürich, Switzerland.

Distributed in the United States by North-South Books Inc., New York.

Library of Congress Cataloging-in-Publication Data is available.
ISBN 1-55858-185-5 (TRADE BINDING)
ISBN 1-55858-186-3 (LIBRARY BINDING)
British Library Cataloguing in Publication Data
Scheidl, Gerda Marie
Loretta and the Little Fairy
I. Title II. James, J. Alison
III. Unzner-Fischer, Christa
833.914 [J]
ISBN 1-55858-185-5

1 3 5 7 9 10 8 6 4 2
Printed in Belgium

Contents

A Real Fairy?

LORETTA lived in a cottage with her mother. She had no one to play with except her doll, Annabella. A little girl named Karen lived next door, but Loretta didn't like her very much. She preferred to play alone.

One day Loretta took Annabella out to the garden. There was a tattered old sofa behind the blackberry bushes that was their special place to play. She put Annabella on the bench and sat down next to her.

"Ouch!" came a voice that sounded like a small bell. Loretta jumped back up and looked around, but she couldn't see anybody. She was sure somebody had said "Ouch." Not loudly, but Loretta had heard it quite clearly.

Loretta listened. It was oddly still in the garden. Only the bees were droning.

"I must have imagined it," she said to herself, and she sat down again.

"Ow! Watch out, would you?" went the ringing voice. Loretta jumped up again and turned around.

"Oh!" she said. There was a girl sitting on the old sofa.

"Did you say 'Ouch'?" asked Loretta.

"Yes," said the girl. "Don't you think it hurts when you sit on someone?"

"What do you mean? You weren't there."

"You just didn't see me," said the little girl. "I was invisible."

"Invisible?" Loretta was astonished.

"Fairies are always invisible at first."

"Are you a fairy? A real fairy?" Loretta asked.

"Well, just a young one," said the fairy.

Loretta smiled. "I've never seen a fairy like you, with scraggly hair and jeans! In my books the fairies are much more beautiful."

"So what?" said the little fairy. "But
anyway, I'll look different when I'm
grown up."

Loretta shook her head. "I don't believe
you are a fairy at all."

The little fairy looked surprised. "Watch,
I'll show you." She pursed her lips and blew
up both cheeks, and then—*whoosh*—she
disappeared!

Loretta looked on the sofa. She
looked under the blackberry bushes. She
even looked in the pear tree. There was
no little girl.

"Hello?" called Loretta.
"Hello!" answered the ringing voice.
Loretta looked around. Nobody.

What Next?

Loretta heard something in the bushes. She turned around and saw the little girl.

"Now do you believe I'm a fairy?"

"Hmm." Loretta wavered. This girl didn't look like a fairy, but fairies *are* magic, and she did make herself disappear.

Loretta nodded. "I believe you."

"Hurrah!" cheered the little fairy.

"What's your name?" Loretta asked.

"Xydaaqe Bowzd," said the little fairy. "But you can call me Fairy."

"What other kinds of magic can you do?" asked Loretta nervously.

The little fairy looked sad. "I can turn myself into a butterfly for a few seconds, but that's it."

"Let me see!" cried Loretta.

"Don't blink. This won't last long!"

Loretta watched in amazement as the little fairy's arms turned into beautiful wings. The fairy hovered in the air for a few seconds and then plunked to the ground.

"Wow," Loretta said. "What else can you do?"

"Nothing. I can't do real magic until I
grow up."

"Why not?" asked Loretta. "I thought all
fairies could do magic."

"It was all because I got into a little
trouble," the little fairy confessed. "I was
angry at another fairy, so I found a little
spell and tried it out. But it didn't work
very well."

"What happened?" asked Loretta, eyes wide.

"I turned her into a glowworm."

Loretta giggled, but she stopped when she saw the little fairy's face.

"I didn't mean to do it," said the little fairy with tears in her eyes. "They sent me to the Supreme Fairy. She told me this—" The little fairy arched her eyebrows and lowered her voice. " 'This nonsense has got to stop. Magic is not something to be taken lightly. I'm sending you to the human world to grow up. Only then will you learn what your real power is.' " The little fairy looked around the garden as if it held an answer. "So that's why I'm here."

"Maybe I'm supposed to help you," said Loretta excitedly. She thought about what might make a fairy grow. "I've got it!" she cried. "You have to eat cherry soup!"

"Eat cherry soup?" asked the little fairy, astonished.

"Yes! My grandpa says cherry soup makes you grow big and strong."

They both ran to find him.

Loretta's grandpa laughed. He cooked up a batch of cherry soup right away.

The little fairy ate four big bowls. Loretta

did too. That was too much. Their stomachs
ached! The little fairy made a face.

"This is no help at all," she snapped at
Loretta. "It hurts!" Before Loretta could say
anything, the little fairy disappeared.

The next day Loretta ran straight out to
the garden to see if the fairy would come
back. She found her crouched in an empty
flowerpot. "Eating cherry soup didn't work,"
she grumbled.

Loretta thought some more. Suddenly
she cried, "I've got it! You have to learn to
read and write! All grown-ups can read
and write!"

"Read and write?"

"Of course! Or do you already know how?"

The little fairy shook her head. "No, I
have no idea."

"I already can," said Loretta proudly. "At
least a little. I'm learning in school."

"Great!" The little fairy jumped up out of the flowerpot. "I want to learn to read and write too! Can you take me with you to school?"

"You? A fairy? Certainly not." Loretta shook her head.

"Certainly so! Certainly so!" sang the little fairy happily.

Mr. Summerpen

And it really worked. The little fairy came
to school with Loretta the next day.

"My name is Fairy," she said to Loretta's
teacher. "I want to learn to read and write."

Mr. Summerpen was so amazed that he
couldn't think of what to say. Then the little
fairy looked at him with her remarkably

bright eyes, and he just gave a friendly nod.

"Thank you," said the little fairy, and she sat down next to Loretta.

Karen, who lived next door to Loretta, smiled shyly at the little fairy. Loretta glared at Karen and gave the little fairy a pen and a notebook. "This is what you write with," she whispered.

Fairies can learn new things in an instant. So the little fairy was soon bored. She yawned loudly while the teacher was giving a spelling test. And then—*whoosh*—she disappeared! Uh oh.

Mr. Summerpen rubbed his eyes. Where was Loretta's friend? Had she crawled under her desk? The teacher went over to her desk and looked. Nothing!

The teacher went back to his desk. Loretta giggled. "Stop giggling!" he said sternly as he sat down.

"Ouch!" A ringing voice sounded from behind him.

Mr. Summerpen jumped up.

Now the whole class was laughing.

The little fairy was sitting on the teacher's chair. "So that's where you are," he said, angrily shaking his head. He was going to scold her, but when she looked at him with those remarkably bright eyes, he just went on with the test. Everybody wrote busily.

The little fairy went back to her seat and started writing.

Baking a Cake

"Are you going to be grown up soon?"
Loretta asked the little fairy when she met
her the next afternoon in the garden.

"No. Not for a long time," said the little
fairy sadly.

She sat on the swing that Loretta's
grandpa had hung in the pear tree.

"But why not?" asked Loretta. "You can already read and write. A lot better than I can."

"But the Supreme Fairy said that wasn't enough."

"What could it be that you still need to learn? Maybe cake baking, or . . ."

"Cake baking? What is that?"

Loretta was amazed. The little fairy didn't even know what baking a cake was!

"My mother bakes a super tremendous cake with raisins! Mmmm, it is delicious!"

"And your mother, is she already grown?" asked the little fairy nervously.

"What a silly question! My mother has been a grown-up her whole life."

"Ooowheeee . . ." The little fairy shouted with joy. "I want to learn to bake a cake. Then finally I will be grown up!" cried the little fairy.

"And then will you cast spells with a magic wand and say magic words and even fly?" cried Loretta.

"Magic wand, magic words, soar like a butterfly—anything I want. Wheeee!"

The little fairy swung higher and higher and higher until she finally disappeared.

Loretta looked around.

Where had the little fairy gone this time?

Something tugged on Loretta's dress, but when she turned, she didn't see the little fairy.

"Hey, you . . ." It was the little bell voice. "Will your mother teach me how to bake a cake?"

"Of course," said Loretta. "But you have to make yourself visible first!"

"Mama, this is my friend Fairy," said Loretta when they were in the house. "Can you show her how to make a raisin cake?"

"Why not?" said Loretta's mother.

Loretta's mother got everything they needed and put it out on the kitchen table. When it was time to mix the batter, she handed the little fairy an electric mixer. The little fairy looked at the thing nervously. What was she supposed to do with it?

36

Loretta's mother explained to her, "You can whip up the batter in no time with that. It's not hard at all; you just have to hold on tight."

The little fairy still looked worried. But she held on tightly. Then Loretta's mother switched on the mixer.

Oh no! It whizzed and exploded. Sparks sprayed everywhere. Like a wild, kicking donkey, the mixer attacked the bowl. Cake batter splattered the room.

The mixer seemed to have a life of its own. Where was the little fairy? She wasn't there!

Loretta's mother quickly pulled the plug, and Loretta wiped blobs of batter from her eyes.

Had the fairy disappeared again? Loretta heard something and she looked up. The fairy was clinging to the kitchen lamp.

"What happened?" asked Loretta.

"I forgot," said the fairy. "We are not allowed to touch things that work on electricity. Can you help me get down from here?"

Loretta's mother held her arms out and the little fairy let herself fall into them.

"It will be all right," she comforted.

"Now there won't be any cake," cried Loretta, looking in the mixing bowl. There was only a little bit of batter left.

"We'll make some more," said her mother,
and she gave them butter, eggs, sugar, milk,
and flour. Then she tossed in a handful of
raisins.

The little fairy stirred everything together
into a batter—with the wooden spoon, of
course. A short while later the most
delicious cake imaginable emerged from
the oven.

The little fairy, Loretta, and her mother each had a piece. Annabella the doll sat nearby and had cake crumbs tucked in her mouth.

"See, dear," Loretta's mother said to the little fairy. "Baking a cake is easy."

Loretta whispered to the little fairy, "Will you come back to see me now that you have grown up?"

The Big Fight

After school the next day, Loretta ran straight to the garden. She sat on the sofa and waited. I hope the little fairy will come soon, Loretta thought.

But the little fairy wasn't there.

"Maybe she is already a grown-up, like my mother," Loretta whispered to Annabella. "What if she never comes back?"

When Loretta looked up again, the little fairy was standing right in front of her. Loretta blinked in surprise; the little fairy looked just the same as always.

"Aren't you grown up yet?" asked Loretta.

"No." The little fairy hung her head.

"But you already ate cherry soup, learned to read and write, and made a raisin cake."

"So? That's nothing special! The grown fairies said so."

Loretta was angry. "That's not fair! I would like to know just what it is you are supposed to learn!"

"Me too . . ." The little fairy began to sob.

"Please don't cry," said Loretta.

But the little fairy sobbed even louder.

"If you cry, I'll have to cry too. And so will Annabella," sniffed Loretta.

"Hu-huuh!" cried the fairy.

"Boo-hoooh!" cried Loretta.

"Waaaa!" cried Annabella.

Karen, the little girl who lived next door to Loretta, heard this.

She was playing alone by the garden fence. She wondered who was crying, but she couldn't tell. Should she risk going nearer?

When the crying got louder and louder, Karen went into the garden.

"Why . . . why are you crying?" she asked shyly.

Loretta looked up. "None of your
business," she said.

"But . . . if you are crying . . . maybe I
could help you," Karen said quietly.

"You? Stupid Karen? There is no way you
could help!"

"Oh . . ." Karen looked at the ground.

"Why did you call Karen stupid?" asked
the little fairy.

"Because every time somebody asks her
something, she has to think about it a
hundred times before she even answers.
Karen is stupid and that's all there is to it!
Blaah!" Loretta stuck out her tongue at
Karen. "Get out of here!"

Karen's eyes filled with tears. Nobody
liked her. Everyone sent her away. Even
Loretta. Karen looked at the two girls. Then
she turned to go.

"No, wait!" called the little fairy. She jumped up and ran after Karen. "I don't think you are stupid. Really I don't. I think you are very nice. Will you play with me?"

Karen stared at the little fairy. Her mouth made a little O with surprise. No one ever wanted to play with her. Karen nodded.

"Great!" said the little fairy. She took Annabella away from the bewildered Loretta and tugged Karen's arm.

"Here! Annabella wants to play with you too."

"Give my doll back this instant!"
Furiously Loretta grabbed Annabella. "How
could you give her my doll?" she screamed.
"That is so mean. You are awful! I thought
you were my friend!"

"I'm Karen's friend too," said the little
fairy. She took Karen by the hand.

"Pah! Then play all you want with the
crazy nut!" screamed Loretta, and she ran
into her house.

Karen's New Friend

Karen and the little fairy played together every day. Behind the house was a meadow. There they built a house out of branches and leaves.

They dressed up in costumes. Karen was Mrs. Popplemouse and the little fairy was Mr. Ticklebird. They played hide-and-seek and climbed trees, and the little fairy taught Karen how to turn somersaults.

Karen was happy. If only Loretta hadn't run off so angrily! Karen was terribly sorry about that.

"Don't worry," comforted the little fairy. "She will come back soon enough."

And she was right. Loretta really did come back.

At first she just peeked over the garden fence. Then she let Annabella fall on the other side.

The little fairy noticed and said, "Could Karen play with Annabella?"

Loretta really wanted to say no, but oddly enough, she answered, "Yes."

"Finally!" said the little fairy.

Karen looked nervously at Loretta. But Loretta simply picked up Annabella and gave her to Karen.

"I didn't really mean it when I called you a crazy nut and I don't really think you are stupid," apologized Loretta.

"She certainly isn't," said the little fairy.

Little Grown-up Fairy

Now they all played house together.
Annabella was the baby. They dressed her
and fed her daisies. They washed her clothes
and hung them out to dry. And when
Annabella was tired, they told her stories
and sang to her and took turns rocking her
to sleep.

But then the little fairy stood up—and disappeared, right in the middle of the game.

What was happening?

Suddenly, there was an eerie swirling in the air and the sound of many bells. Loretta and Karen looked at each other. When they looked back to where the little fairy had been, they saw the most beautiful girl standing in front of them.

It was the little fairy, but she looked so different.

She waved to the two girls.

"Good-bye," she said softly. "Thank you for helping me grow up!"

Then she slowly faded away.

Karen squeezed Loretta's hand. "What happened to the little fairy?"

"I guess she grew up," whispered Loretta. "All the little fairy wanted was to grow up fast, so she could do magic. That's why she ate the cherry soup, and learned to read and write and to bake a cake." Loretta paused, and then she continued. "But she had to do something special."

"So what did she do?" asked Karen.

"Who knows?" Loretta shrugged. Then she said thoughtfully, "I never wanted to play with you, even though you are nice." She looked at Karen. "Maybe that's it. Maybe she put a spell on us so we could play together. That must be what she did."

"Maybe," agreed Karen, "but I don't think it was magic. She was just nice. And brave. Do you think she'll come back?"

"I hope so," said Loretta. "Think of all the fun we could have if she could cast spells, say magic words, and fly!"

"What should we do now?" asked Karen.

"Well," said Loretta cheerfully. "You can pretend to be the little fairy, and I'll teach you how to grow up."

"What do we do first?"

"Eat cherry soup!" cried Loretta.

About the Illustrator

Christa Unzner-Fischer was born in a small town near Berlin, in what was then part of East Germany. She wanted to become a ballet dancer, but she ended up studying commercial art and working in an advertising agency. She entered a book illustration contest and won third prize, which led to a career as a free-lance illustrator, primarily of children's books. She loves fairy tales and fantasy stories, especially books like *Alice's Adventures in Wonderland*. Christa Unzner-Fischer is married and lives in Berlin.

About the Author

Gerda Marie Scheidl was born in a small town in Germany. While she was studying dance and acting in Vienna, she married Otto Scheidl, an opera singer. She worked for many years as a dancer, and then became the manager of a children's theatre. She was the stage director, designed the costumes and sets, and wrote the plays. Later she began writing fairy tales and children's books. She loves to tell stories, and when she reads aloud from her books, it is like a small theatrical performance.

About the Translator

J. Alison James was born in southern California but has had many adventures in northern Germany. She studied German and Swedish so she would be able to translate the extraordinary children's books published in those languages. She believes that in books children can discover how similar people are all over the world.

Alison James has also written two young adult novels, *Sing for a Gentle Rain* and *Runa*. She lives with her husband and young daughter in Vermont, where the blackberry bushes tangle with the delphiniums and the fairies are nearly always visible.